Hello Baldwin!

Aimee Aryal

Illustrated by Tai Hwa Goh

MASCOT BOOKS™

www.mascotbooks.com

It was a beautiful fall day at
Boston College.

Baldwin was on his way to
Alumni Stadium to watch
a football game.

He walked through O'Neill Plaza.

A group of students studying there
waved, "Hello Baldwin!"

Baldwin passed by Bapst Library.

A professor walking by said,
"Hello Baldwin!"

Baldwin went over to
St. Ignatius Church.

A priest standing outside the church
waved, "Hello Baldwin!"

On the way to the game, Baldwin stopped at Conte Forum where the Eagles play hockey and basketball.

A group of BC fans standing nearby
yelled, "Hello Baldwin!"

It was almost time for the football game.
As Baldwin walked to the stadium,
he passed by some alumni.

The alumni remembered Baldwin from
when they went to Boston College.
They said, "Hello, again, Baldwin!"

Finally, Baldwin arrived at
Alumni Stadium.

As he ran onto the football field,
the crowd cheered, "Let's Go Eagles!"

Baldwin watched the game from
the sidelines and cheered
for the team.

The Eagles scored six points!
The quarterback shouted,
"Touchdown Baldwin!"

At half-time the Boston College Band
performed on the field.

Baldwin and the crowd sang,
"For Boston."

The Boston College Eagles won
the football game!

Baldwin gave Coach O'Brien
a high-five. The coach said,
"Great game Baldwin!"

After the football game, Baldwin was
tired. It had been a long day
at Boston College.

He walked home and climbed into bed.

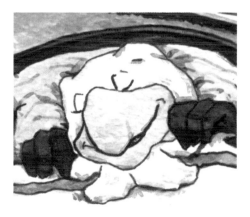

"Goodnight Baldwin."

For Anna and Maya,
and all of Baldwin's little fans. ~ AA

To my Mom and Daddy. ~ THG

Special thanks to:

Tom O'Brien

Brad Truman

For information please contact Mascot Books,
P.O. Box 220157, Chantilly, VA 20153-0157.

BOSTON COLLEGE, BOSTON COLLEGE EAGLES, EAGLES, B.C. and B.C. EAGLES
are trademarks or registered trademarks of Boston College and are used under license.

ISBN: 1-932888-13-6

Printed in the United States.

www.mascotbooks.com